RIDER WOOFSON

THE CASE OF THE MISSING TIGER'S EYE

BY WALKER STYLES ● ILLUSTRATED BY BEN WHITEHOUSE

LITTLE SIMON

New York   London   Toronto   Sydney   New Delhi

LITTLE SIMON

An imprint of Simon & Schuster Children's Publishing Division
1230 Avenue of the Americas, New York, New York 10020
First Little Simon hardcover edition January 2016
Copyright © 2016 by Simon & Schuster, Inc.
Also available in a Little Simon paperback edition.
All rights reserved, including the right of reproduction in whole or in part in any form.
LITTLE SIMON is a registered trademark of Simon & Schuster, Inc., and associated colophon is a trademark of Simon & Schuster, Inc. For information about special discounts for bulk purchases, please contact Simon & Schuster Special Sales at 1-866-506-1949 or business@simonandschuster.com. The Simon & Schuster Speakers Bureau can bring authors to your live event. For more information or to book an event contact the Simon & Schuster Speakers Bureau at 1-866-248-3049 or visit our website at www.simonspeakers.com. Designed by Laura Roode.
The text of this book was set in ITC American Typewriter.
Manufactured in the United States of America 1215 FFG
2 4 6 8 10 9 7 5 3 1
Library of Congress Cataloging-in-Publication Data
Styles, Walker.
The case of the missing Tiger's Eye / by Walker Styles ; illustrated by Ben Whitehouse. — First Little Simon paperback edition.
pages cm — (Rider Woofson ; 1)
ISBN 978-1-4814-5738-5 (hc) — ISBN 978-1-4814-5739-2 (pbk) — ISBN 978-1-4814-5740-8 (eBook) [1. Mystery and detective stories.
2. Detectives—Fiction. 3. Dogs—Fiction. 4. Animals—Fiction.
5. Sculpture—Fiction.] I. Whitehouse, Ben, illustrator. II. Title.
PZ7.1.S82Cas 2016
[Fic]—dc23
2015009103

CONTENTS

Chapter 1	Welcome to Pawston	1
Chapter 2	A Shadow Surprise	15
Chapter 3	Where's Westie?	27
Chapter 4	A <u>Hiss</u>-terical Owner	37
Chapter 5	Slippery Clues	49
Chapter 6	The Banana Splits	63
Chapter 7	Monkey Business	75
Chapter 8	Who's Chasing Whom?!	87
Chapter 9	A Barrel Full of Bad Guys	99
Chapter 10	The Last Laugh	111

WELCOME TO PAWSTON

🐾

Rider Woofson stared out of his office window, looking over the city skyline. Buildings stretched out for miles in every direction. This was Pawston, the animal capital of the world. Every day, thousands of animals went about their business, behaving as good citizens should.

But this city also had a darker side, known as the criminal under-belly. And it was not the kind of belly you wanted to scratch. Not unless you wanted to get bit!

That was where Rider Woofson came in. Rider was no ordinary canine. He was the greatest dog detective in Pawston—maybe even the world. And with the help of his pals in the Pup Investigators Pack, criminals didn't stand a chance.

In fact, the only problem for the P.I. Pack was waiting for an actual crime to happen.

"Well, it's been a pretty quiet afternoon, huh, Boss?" said Westie Barker.

"It is quiet," Rider woofed. "Too quiet." He fixed his crooked tie and

adjusted his hat. "I don't like it."

"A day off must be *terrier*-fying for a working dog like you," the West Highland terrier said with a laugh. He was fiddling with a screwdriver and what used to be a vacuum cleaner. "Try to enjoy it. You could grab a dognap or buy a

new collar. Maybe play a game of fetch?"

"We're not pups anymore," Rider said, looking over his friend's shoulder. "Say, what is that?"

"It's my new toy project . . . a jetpack!" Westie said as he wagged his tail. The white-furred terrier was a true gadget expert. He was always building something new. "With this strapped to my back, I'll be able to solve crimes faster than a speeding greyhound."

"I bet that jetpack won't get one foot off the ground," Rora Gooddog

said from across the room. She
was the prettiest poodle on the
block, and twice as smart. She
was sitting at her desk, writing up
a crime report.

"Flying is for the birds anyways," said a floppy-haired mutt named Ziggy Fluffenscruff. "I like to keep my paws on the ground, thank you very much." The young pup sniffed around the office. He followed his nose over to the file cabinet. After digging through a

few papers, he pulled out a bone
and hugged it. *"Bow-wowza!"* he
yipped. "I knew you weren't lost."

"So you're the one who put
bite marks on this," Rora said as
she grabbed the bone back and

returned it to the file cabinet. "This is evidence, not dinner. Now, quit thinking with your stomach."

"Thinking with my stomach has helped solve lots of cases, you know," Ziggy whispered to himself, curling up on the couch. "Like that one with the mean dog magician, Labra-cadabra-dor."

"Kid, you've got a real talent there," Rider said. "And I bet your nose could smell trouble a mile away."

"Trouble?" said Ziggy, the youngest of the P.I. Pack. "No, thanks. I'd rather sniff out pup-peroni pizza and super-duper sandwiches with pup-pickles on top."

As Ziggy continued to talk about food, Rider looked out the window again. The bright lights of Pawston twinkled beneath him, but the city outside was still too quiet. And Rider knew exactly what that meant. Somewhere out there, the P.I. Pack's next case was about to unfold.

A SHADOW SURPRISE

🐾

Mr. Meow stared into the eyes of a tiger. He shivered—not from fright, but from delight. He had never seen anything so beautiful in his life! For this wasn't a real tiger, but rather a small golden *sculpture* of a tiger that had two giant gems for its eyes.

"Neat statue," said Frenchie,

the French bulldog security guard.
Frenchie worked for Mr. Meow,
who owned a new jewelry store in
Pawston called the Cat's Meow.

"Neat?" Mr. Meow snapped. "I would say it's more than 'neat.' This 'statue' is a world-famous piece of art called the Tiger's Eye. The sculpture is *meow*-nificent, and those gems are worth millions."

"Millions?!" Frenchie gulped. "I ain't never seen nothin' worth that much."

"Well, you have now," Mr. Meow said. "And I suggest you take extra care to keep a watchful eye tonight. Who knows who might want to steal a thing of such value."

"Then what's it doin' here in your store, Mr. Meow?" Frenchie asked. "Should it be in a museum or somethin' somewhere?"

"It should be, yes," Mr. Meow began to explain. "The Tiger's Eye is on tour across the country. But as the Pawston Museum caught fire last week, I said I'd house this *purr*-fect piece in my fine jewelry store. Tomorrow, we will open the doors for Pawston's finest citizens to come and see such beauty. But for now, *I* need *my* beauty sleep. Good night, Frenchie." Mr. Meow started for the front door.

"Hold up," Frenchie called to his boss. "You don't want to forget this!" The security guard gave him an umbrella. "It's rainin' cats and dogs out there!"

"It certainly is." Mr. Meow frowned. "This weather is *purr*-fectly awful."

Mr. Meow disappeared into
the stormy downpour. Frenchie
double-checked the doors to make
sure they were locked up tight.

After making his first rounds, Frenchie took a seat to watch his favorite scary movie: *Franken-Pooch*. But around ten o'clock, a dark shadow floated across the skylight. "Is someone there?" he asked, turning on his flashlight.

A quiet *swish* sounded above him. Frenchie aimed his flashlight up, but no one was there. A few

seconds later, he heard another *swish*. His ears perked up and he flashed the light in the new direction. Still nothing.

"Guess my imagination is gettin' the best of me," Frenchie said with a smile, shutting off his flashlight. "Probably just the wind."

But as Frenchie turned to leave, a shadow appeared on the wall. At first, the shadow was the size of a small pup, but then it began to grow taller, and taller, and taller, and taller. . . .

25

WHERE'S WESTIE?

🐾

thing warms my paws like a
cup of tea in the morning,"
said as she poured herself
hot water.

gy was busy making a stack
ead, eggs, cheese, ketchup,
dry dog food, and then
bread.

a looked at Ziggy and shook

her head. "Hey, kid. What are you doing?"

"Making a work of art," Ziggy said proudly. "There's nothing better than a breakfast sandwich with extra kibble."

He lifted the massive sandwich into the air. But before he could take a bite, Rider flung open the office door and hit the sandwich. Eggs, bacon, and kibble splashed all over poor Ziggy.

"My masterpiece . . . ," he whimpered.

"That's right, Ziggy," Rider Woofson said. "A masterpiece has been stolen!" Rider held up a copy of the *Pawston Paw Print*, the town newspaper. The first five pages were all about the theft of the Tiger's Eye sculpture. "I smell

a mystery, P.I. Pack," Rider said.
"I also smell bacon."

Ziggy sniffed at his breakfast
sandwich all over the floor. He
began scraping bits and pieces
back onto a plate.

"The whole team needs to be ready to go if we get the call," Rider said, grabbing his magnifying glass from his desk. "Speaking of the whole team, where's Westie?"

As if to answer Rider's question,

Westie crashed through the window and began flying around the
room in a large circle. "I'm flying!"
Westie cried out over the roar of
his jetpack.

"Hey, birdbrain, get your feet on the ground!" Rider said. "Before you hit the—"

But it was too late. Westie hit the ceiling fan, which sent him crashing into Ziggy and his almost-fixed sandwich.

Rora laughed at Westie and Ziggy. "Hope you boys are as good at cleaning up as you are at making a mess."

"I'll clean up later," Westie said, already fiddling with his jetpack.

"First, I need to figure out if the problem with the thruster output is caused by—"

"What about my breakfast? Someone needs to make sure I get fed," Ziggy whined.

Rider was about to tell his P.I. Pack to get it together when the phone rang. The detective picked it up on the first ring. "What can I help you with, Mr. Mayor?

I see. We'll be right there." As soon
as he hung up, Rider grabbed his
hat and announced,
"The P.I. Pack is
officially on the
case. Let's go!"

A
<u>HISS</u>-TeRICAL
OWNeR

Mr. Meow snarled. "I am *hiss-
terical* with anger!"

"It's going to be okay," the
mayor said, trying to calm the
upset store owner.

"How will it be okay?" Mr. Meow
asked. "My store has been broken
into, my guard has been fright-
ened halfway to the end of his

leash, and the Tiger's Eye sculpture has been stolen! My reputa-
tion is ruined!"

"I believe that's where we come
in," Rider said, arriving with Rora
and Ziggy. They appeared from
the large crowd of animals that
had gathered to see what had

happened. Rider took off his hat and offered a polite nod.

"Mr. Meow, meet Rider Woofson, Pawston's finest detective," the mayor said. "If anyone can find the missing sculpture, it's him and the P.I. Pack."

"Let us hope so," Mr. Meow said. "Otherwise, I'll be crying over more than spilled milk." With that, Mr. Meow stormed off.

"Mr. Mayor, I'd like to get started if you don't mind," Rider said, always ready to get down to business. "First, I would like to speak with the security guard."

Frenchie was shaken up, but he was happy to help. Rider asked him to describe the event exactly as he remembered it.

"Everything was fine until just after ten o'clock," Frenchie began.

"That's when the noises started. I went to see who was there, and then I saw it. . . . It was a giant shadow, I swear! I didn't see a face, but it musta stood at least twenty feet tall!"

"*Bow-wowza!*" Ziggy said. "A shadow giant! That's like something out of a scary movie!"

"Like *Franken-Pooch!*" Frenchie said, his eyes getting wide. "Do you think it's possible that a monster stole the Tiger's Eye?"

"I do not," Rora said matter-of-factly.

"Mr. Frenchie, thanks for your time." Rider walked away and the Pack followed. "Sounds like someone got scared watching a silly

movie and is wagging a tall tale.
Now let's go check inside for clues."

"Where's Westie?" Ziggy asked.
"He's always skipping all the hard
work."

"Right up there, kid." Rora pointed up at the sky. A small speck was making circles over the jewelry store.

"I can't get down!" Westie barked from above.

"Make like a cat and land on your feet!" Ziggy shouted.

"Quit fooling around, Westie," Rider said. "We have a crime to solve."

But as Rider and his team moved into the jewelry store, he glanced back at the onlookers.

A mean-looking rottweiler was standing at the edge of the crowd. The fur on the back of Rider's neck stood up. He had a bad feeling about that dog. And Rider always trusted his instincts.

SLIPPERY CLUES

🐾

"A gal could get used to this kind of scenery," Rora said inside the jewelry store. She was admiring all the gold and jewels. "Think the owner will pay us in diamonds? After all, diamonds are a dog's best friend."

"We don't do our work for the money. We do it for justice," Rider said. He sniffed around for clues.

"I do it for the kibble and cookies," Ziggy said. "Ooh, this is shiny. . . ." Ziggy was reaching out to touch a large diamond when Rora swatted him away.

"No touching, kid," Rora said. "Not until after we dust for paw prints."

"Well, no sign of forced entry at any of the doors or windows," Rider said as he checked the exits. "Mr. Meow keeps this place locked up as tight as an obedience school."

"So what are you saying?" Ziggy asked. "The

Tiger's Eye just vanished? Maybe it really was a giant shadow monster?!" Ziggy started to get excited at the idea of a real monster—then he got scared.

"It wasn't a monster, kid," Rora said, rolling her eyes.

"There must be a good explanation around here somewhere," Rider said, rubbing his jaw and scanning the room.

"While you try to figure that out, I am going to grab

a bite to—*whoa!*" Ziggy suddenly slipped, flipped, and landed upside down. "Why is the room upside down?" Ziggy asked.

Rider put on a glove and picked up the banana peel stuck to Ziggy's

foot. "You just slipped on our first clue," Rider said with a smile. "Good job, Zig."

"A banana peel and no banana? No fair," Ziggy said, sniffing at the clue. "Hey, I know where this banana came from! They grow on trees in Central Bark Park."

"That's some nose you got, kid," Rora said.

"Thank you! I never ever forget a—*whoa!*" Ziggy slipped, flipped, and landed on his back. "Smell. Ouch. That did not feel good."

"You found another banana peel?" Rider asked.

"No, I slipped in a puddle this time," said Ziggy. "A puddle of monster drool! See? It *is* a monster!"

Rider bent down and licked the water. "That's not drool—that's rainwater . . . from last night's storm." Rider looked up. "Looks like someone came in through that open skylight."

"A banana peel and a skylight? How do those fit together?" Rora asked, thinking out loud.

"Watch out, everybody!" Westie shouted. He zoomed in through the skylight. His jetpack was smoking but still flying.

"Westie, fly outside, or you are going to make a mess of the crime scene!" Rider shouted.

"Aye, aye, I'll try, Captain!" said Westie, zipping over their heads.

"But this jetpack has a mind of its own!" Westie steered himself out through the front door, just missing a giant jewelry case filled with diamonds and rubies. Two seconds later, there was a loud *CRASH!*

The rest of the P.I. Pack rushed out of the Cat's Meow to see what had happened. Westie flew over the crowd and across the street, where he crashed into a big sign above the Pawston Theater. "I'm okay," he moaned.

"Well, would you look at that,"
Rider said. The sign out front read:

Ziggy and Rora followed Rider's
gaze. "Clue number three?" Rora
asked.

"Grab a nice suit when you
get down, Westie," Rider hollered.
"Tonight, we're going to a show!"

"Sounds like a plan," Westie
answered from above and waved
his paw in the air.

THEATER

chapter
SIX

FINAL SHOW
SOLD OUT
FINAL SPLITS

THE BANANA SPLITS

"Let me get that for you," Rora said to Rider as she helped fix his bow tie. The entire P.I. Pack was dressed up for the theater.

"Keep your eyes peeled," Rider said as he guided Rora, Ziggy, and Westie to their seats. "If my hunch is right, we're about to meet the thieves who stole the Tiger's Eye."

"Who cares about thieves—this popcorn is amazing!" Ziggy said, chewing with his mouth open.

"I'm excited to use these mega 3-D binoculars I built last month. I can see every inch of the stage from here," Westie said, fiddling with little dials and knobs on a

rather large pair of metal goggles
he was wearing.

"*Shhh*, the show is starting."
Rora hushed the others.

The lights dimmed, and a dozen
monkeys lowered themselves from
the top of the stage. Hand in foot,
each monkey formed a link in a

chain. "That's how they got into the store through the skylight," Rora whispered. "Teamwork."

The show continued as the Banana Splits did one trick after another, performing all kinds of amazing acrobatic and aerial feats. Then the monkeys jumped on one another's shoulders to form one giant body. They walked across the stage as one unit. "The shadow giant!" Ziggy said.

Westie handed Rider his mega 3-D binoculars. "Put these on."

"Not now," Rider said.

"Trust me, you'll want to see this."

Rider put on the goggles and looked to where Westie pointed. At the back of the stage, something shimmered in the dark. Rider

adjusted the binoculars, and the Tiger's Eye sculpture came into focus. "They have the statue!" Rider exclaimed. But as he stood up, someone else in the crowd did too—the scary-looking rottweiler.

The rottweiler ran down the aisle and disappeared behind the

side curtain. "After him!" Rider
said to his P.I. Pack.

"But my popcorn!" Ziggy cried
as Westie dragged him behind
Rora toward the stage.

"There he goes!" yelled Rider,
pointing at the rottweiler. The

rottweiler was just about to grab the Tiger's Eye, but the monkeys got to it first. A dozen monkeys ran all over the stage, tossing the statue back and forth to one another.

"They're playing keep-away with the statue!" Ziggy shouted.

"Catch them!" ordered Rora, but the monkeys were too fast. They jumped all over the place. They climbed the rafters, passing the statue back and forth, until they reached the catwalk. Then they took a bow, and the crowd applauded. The audience

thought this was all part
of the final act.

"We have fans!" Ziggy waved.

"But this show is
just getting started!"
Rider shouted.

Monkey Business

🐾

The monkeys rode down on the large red curtain and surrounded Rider and the P.I. Pack. The golden statue with gems for eyes flew through the air again and again as the furry crooks continued to toss it back and forth. Suddenly, the rottweiler swung in on a rope and tried to grab the Tiger's Eye, but the Banana Splits knocked him aside and ran away.

"Let's split up!" roared Rora. "Rider, take care of the rottweiler! We'll get that statue."

Rider chased the rottweiler. "Sit, boy! Sit!" he commanded.

The rottweiler growled. "The name's Rotten Ruffhouse, Detective. And I don't do tricks!"

"You're a bad dog," Rider said as he leaped onto the mysterious mutt's back. But Rotten shook him off and disappeared into another doorway with Rider right behind him.

Meanwhile, the rest of the P.I. Pack chased the monkeys into a dressing room. But as soon as the Pack entered, there was no sign of the Banana Splits. "Be careful, boys," Rora said. "They've got to be in here somewhere."

Rora saw a monkey tail peeking out from under a large wig. She

grabbed it, and a monkey jumped into the air with a screech. Then five other monkeys popped out from behind more props, holding rainbow wigs. They heaved wig after wig on top of Rora until she was buried under a hairy pile. "Help! I'm wigging out!" she cried.

Across the room,
Westie was searching
through a rack of
clothes when two
monkeys surprised him
in a tangle of costumes.
Before Westie could
react, the monkeys
had him all tied
up and dangled
him all the way
down to the
parking lot.

Ziggy had found the kitchen next door. Of course getting the statue back was important, but his stomach was growling. "There has to be food in here," he said. He peered inside a cabinet and four more monkeys were hiding there! They hollered and pushed Ziggy out of the way. One of them had the Tiger's Eye.

"Hey, you funky monkeys, give me that!" Ziggy said. But as he fumbled forward, a monkey tripped him, and he fell headfirst into a gigantic cream pie.

"That was a waste of a perfectly good pie!" Ziggy shouted angrily.

Then all twelve monkeys began leaping onto one another's backs until they formed the shadow giant. "Uh-oh," Ziggy squeaked.

Next they formed a large fist and were about to crush Ziggy when Westie zoomed in with his jetpack and picked up his friend.

"I thought I was a goner!" Ziggy cried.

"You still might be!" Westie shouted as he lost control of the jetpack. The pair turned midair and crashed into the shadow giant.

Westie, Ziggy, and the monkeys went flying in all directions. Then the statue fell to the ground in the middle of the room. Everyone looked at the Tiger's Eye.

But before anyone could move to get it, Rotten ran through the room, scooped up the treasure, and ran out the exit.

Rider was just
a few feet behind
the thief. "Anyone want to help
me put this crook in a kennel?"
he shouted at the P.I. Pack. The
monkeys and dogs all ran out
the exit, everyone chasing the
statue.

chapter
EIGHT

WHO'S CHASING WHOM?!

🐾

Rotten hopped onto his motorcycle and roared down the street.

"After him!" Rider shouted to his P.I. Pack as they all jumped into their van. Rider hit the gas, and the van sped off after the thief and the Tiger's Eye.

"What about those monkeys? Shouldn't we be after them?"

Westie asked from the backseat.

"Right now, we need to get that priceless statue back," Rider said, turning the steering wheel. "Those monkeys have probably split."

"Wrong, Rider." Ziggy gulped.

"The Banana Splits are hot on our tails." Coming up behind the P.I. Pack van was a tiny car filled with the monkey troupe. One of the monkeys took a single banana peel and hurled it at the van.

Then an explosion of peels flew toward their van!

"Watch out!" Rora shouted, but it was too late. The van slid on the banana peels and started spinning. Then the monkeys hurled a banana cream pie that hit the van's windshield with a messy *smack*.

"I can't see a thing!" Rider shouted as he tried to drive the van. The monkeys zoomed by, gaining on Rotten Ruffhouse and the Tiger's Eye.

"I can help with that!" Ziggy cheered. Faster than a cheetah,

he leaped out of the car and licked the van's windshield clean. "*Bow-wowza!* I love banana cream pie!"

"Back inside, Ziggy," Rider said as he punched the gas.

"Good job, kid. Guess we owe your stomach a thanks." Rora smiled.

"Or a treat!" Ziggy said.

"You cannot still be hungry, can you?" asked Rora.

"Always!" Ziggy said, licking his paws clean.

The P.I. Pack was back on the road and quickly catching up to the others. The monkeys fired banana blasts at Rotten, but he dodged them with ease.

Then the side window opened on the monkey car. One by one, the monkeys hopped on one another's shoulders until they formed a giant arm. The tiny car sped next to the motorcycle as the arm arched over. It grabbed the Tiger's Eye!

Rotten held on to the statue, but he took his eyes off the road. His motorcycle flew up a ramp and into the air, landing with a big splash in the City Kitty River.

"Holy guacamole!" Ziggy said. "Those monkeys have stolen the statue again!"

"Enough of this monkey business," Rider growled.

The Banana Splits' car took a

fast left turn and parked in front of Central Bark Park. Rider made the turn too, zooming after them.

"Uh-oh," Westie said. "What are they doing now?"

The Banana Splits grabbed a tree branch in the park. All twelve monkeys and the Tiger's Eye went swinging into the leaves.

"They are monkeying around in the trees!" Ziggy moaned. "We'll never find them in this giant park now!"

"Sure, we will," said Rider as he pulled the van over. "We've got them right where we want them."

chapter
NINE

A BARREL FULL OF BAD GUYS

🐾

"How are we going to get those monkeys before they sell the Tiger's Eye at the underground flea market?" Ziggy whined.

"With our team genius," Rider said, looking at Westie. "Your jet-pack is made from a vacuum cleaner, right?"

"It sure is!" Westie smiled and

his ears perked up. "You think I'm a genius?"

"Don't let it go to your head," Rider said with a smirk. "Can I borrow your jetpack?"

"You sure can, Boss!" Westie said proudly as he helped Rider put it on.

"Rora and Westie, head back to the river and see if you can find that rottweiler," said Rider. "Ziggy and I are going to get those monkeys *and* the Tiger's Eye."

"Me?" Ziggy gulped. "Uh-uh, no way, José. Vacuum cleaners and I do *not* get along!"

"Time to face your fears, kid," Rider said, grabbing Ziggy and blasting into the air high above the trees.

"Can't I do that on the ground where it's safe?" Ziggy whined.

"This is pretty fun, huh?" Rider
shouted over the wind.

"No, no, and no!" Ziggy cried,
his paws over his eyes.

"Ziggy," said Rider, "you're the
only one who can tell me where
those banana trees are . . . like
that banana we found at the crime

scene. It's up to you to solve this whole case."

"It is?" Ziggy said, his ears perking up and his tail starting to wag.

"It is," Rider said. "Now let's go bananas!"

"*Bow-wowza*, this isn't so bad!"

Ziggy slowly opened his eyes. "There are the banana trees!"

Underneath the flying dogs, there were trees filled with yellow bananas, bustling with hidden monkeys.

Rider broke off one of the jetpack's rockets and flipped the switch from mega-blast to mega-suction mode. The giant vacuum came to life and began sucking at the trees. At first, only bananas and leaves filled up the clear tank, but then, one by one, the monkeys were sucked in too! The

final monkey flew through the air
holding the Tiger's Eye, but Rider
snatched it away safely.

"We got 'em all!" Ziggy shouted.
"*Dog*-gone it, that was fun!"

Rider and Ziggy flew out of the

park and toward the river.
They landed beside the P.I.
Pack van, where Rora and
Westie were waiting.

"The rottweiler got away," Rora said. "His wet paw prints lead up to the road, and then they end. Someone must have picked him up. That means he wasn't working alone."

"Sounds like a mystery for

another day, Rora," Rider said. All the monkeys were pressed against the glass. "Today, we saved the Tiger's Eye—and nabbed a barrel full of bad guys."

THE LAST LAUGH

🐾

"Mr. Meow, I believe this belongs to you," Rider said, handing the store owner the Tiger's Eye statue in time for the opening.

"*Thissss h-issss* outrageous—" Mr. Meow started to hiss, before calming down and finishing, "—ly wonderful. How did you find my, er, I mean, the tour's treasure?"

"A simple crime, really," Rider began. "After their show ended at ten o'clock, the Banana Splits crossed the street, climbed in through the skylight of the Cat's Meow Jewelry Store, and formed a giant shadow to scare the guard dog away. But one of the monkeys took a snack break. He left a clue behind—a banana peel. After that, it was just simple detective work. Just a typical dog day afternoon," Rider said. "With some extra help from my friends," he added, nodding to his teammates.

Rider pointed to the barrel full of monkeys on top of the van. "I believe your police force can take these monkeys off our back, Mr. Mayor?"

"They most certainly can, Rider Woofson." The mayor smiled and shook the detective's paw. "Once

again, Pawston is in your debt."

"Not at all, Mr. Mayor. I'm just glad the P.I. Pack was here to help."

A crowd had appeared and started to cheer. The Tiger's Eye exhibit could start on time, and the whole town was ready to line up to see the amazing treasure. Mr. Meow handed the statue to Frenchie the guard dog and disappeared into his back office.

"I sssssmell a wet dog. Come here, Rotten Ruffhouse, and explain yoursssself," Mr. Meow hissed.

The soaked rottweiler stepped out of the shadows. "It wasn't my fault, Boss," he said. "Those monkeys double-crossed us. They wanted to keep the Tiger's Eye for themselves. I was about to take it when that *dog*-gone P.I. Pack got involved."

"It looks like my *purrr*-fect plan wasn't so *purrr*-fect after all," Mr. Meow said, digging his claws into a golden scratching post.

"Sorry, Boss," Rotten whined.

"Evil help is *ssso* hard to find these days*ssss*," Mr. Meow hissed. "Never send a dog to do a cat's job."

Mr. Meow climbed to the top of the scratching post and stared out the window over the city of Pawston. "Such a big city, and so much crime to be had. I'll have to keep an eye on this P.I. Pack. They could *ssss*pell trouble for my evil plans."

Then Mr. Meow began to laugh a scary, mean laugh. His laughter grew louder, and louder, and louder, and floated out through the window, echoing through Pawston.

The city streets weren't quiet anymore.

CHECK OUT RIDER WOOFSON'S NEXT CASE!

"What in Pawston is going on?" Rider Woofson barked. The dog detective was driving his P.I. Pack to their favorite diner to celebrate solving their latest case. But cars were bumper to bumper, and the traffic wasn't moving. Rider didn't like sitting still, not when he could be solving a crime.

Excerpt from *Something Smells Fishy*

"Maybe I can see what's happening with my new Seeing Eye Dog Glasses," Westie Barker said, wagging his tail excitedly. Westie adjusted his homemade periscope that was raised over the traffic. "It's a real zoo at the Pawston Marina. Half the city must be there . . . and everyone has cameras. Wonder what all the hubbub is about."

"The marina?" Rora Gooddog looked up from her book. "Is it Tuesday already? I almost forgot about Prince Bubbles."

Excerpt from *Something Smells Fishy*

"Who's Prince Bubbles?" Westie asked.

"If he's not a super sub sandwich with mayo and extra marshmallows, who cares? I'm hungry!" Ziggy whined.

"Prince Bubbles is fish royalty," Rora answered, "from the underwater country of New Sealand."

"Hey, isn't that the prince who hardly ever leaves the water? I wonder what brings him to dry land," Rider said, parking the P.I. van. "I'd like to go investigate. You've caught my curiosity."

Excerpt from *Something Smells Fishy*